BLOOD
ROSES

Francesca Lia Block

BLOOD
ROSES

JOANNA COTLER BOOKS

An Imprint of HarperCollins*Publishers*

HARPER TEEN

"Blood Roses" was originally published in *Firebirds Rising:
An Anthology of Original Science Fiction and Fantasy,*
edited by Sharyn November (Firebird, 2006).

Library of Congress Cataloging-in-Publication Data
Block, Francesca Lia.
Blood roses / Francesca Lia Block. — 1st ed.
      p.   cm.
Summary: A collection of magic realist stories of transforma-
tion.
"'Blood Roses' is reprinted from *Firebirds Rising: An Anthology
of Original Science Fiction and Fantasy*, published in 2006 by
Firebird, an imprint of Penguin Group (USA) Inc."—Copyright
p.
Contents: Blood roses — Giant — My haunted house — My
boyfriend is an alien — Horses are a girl's best friend — Skin art
— My mother the vampire — Wounds and wings — Changelings.
ISBN 978-0-06-076384-8 (trade bdg.) — ISBN 978-0-06-
076385-5 (lib. bdg.)
1. Short stories, American. 2. Supernatural—Juvenile fiction. [1. Short stories. 2. Supernatural—Fiction.] I. Title.
PZ7.B61945Blo 2008   2007029564
[Fic]—dc22   CIP
                                                  AC

Typography by Carla Weise
1 2 3 4 5 6 7 8 9 10

First Edition

For all of you…
willing to transform

Also by Francesca Lia Block

BLOOD
ROSES

Contents

Blood Roses

$\mathcal{E}$very day, Lucy and Rosie searched for the blood roses in their canyon. They found eucalyptus and poison oak, evening primrose and oleander but never the glow-in-the-dark red, smoke-scented flowers with sharp thorns that traced poetry onto your flesh.

"You only see them if you die," Lucy said, but Rosie just smiled so that the small row of pearls in her mouth showed.

Still, the hairs stood up on both their fore-
arms and napes that evening, turning them to
furry faunesses for a moment as they sat
watching the sunset from their secret grotto in
the heart of the canyon. The air smelled of
exhaust fumes and decaying leaves. The sky
was streaked with smog and you could hear the
sound of cars and one siren but that world felt
very far away.

Here, the girls turned doll-size, wove nests
out of twigs to sleep in the eucalyptus branches,
collected morning dew in leaves and dined on
dark purple berries that stained their mouths
and hands.

"We'd better get home," Lucy said, brushing the dirt off her jeans.

They would have stayed here all night in
spite of the dangers—snakes, coyote, rapists,

goblins. It was better than the apartment made of tears where their mother had taken them when she left their father.

Their mother said their father was an alcoholic and a sex addict but all Lucy remembered was the sandpaper roughness of his chin, like the father in her baby book *Pat the Bunny*, when he hugged her and Rosie in his arms at the same time. He had hair of blackbird feathers and his eyes were green semiprecious stones.

Lucy and Rosie loved Emerson Solo because like their father he was beautiful, dangerous and unattainable. Especially now. Emerson Solo, twenty-seven, had stabbed himself to death in the heart last month.

You really had to want to die to be successful at that, their mother said before she confiscated all their Solo CDs and posters. Lucy understood why she'd done it. But still she wanted to look at his face and hear his voice again. For some reason he comforted her, even now. Was it because he had escaped?

❧

Lucy and Rosie were in the music store looking through the Emerson Solo discs. There was the one with the black bird on the cover called *For Sorrow* and the one called *The White Room*. There was a rumor that the white room was supposed to be death. The store was all out of *Collected* with the photo of Emerson Solo holding a bouquet of wildflowers with their dirty roots dragging down out of his hands.

A man was standing across the aisle from them and when Lucy looked up he smiled. He was young and handsome with fair hair, a strong chin.

"You like him?" he asked.

Rosie said, "Oh, yes! Our mom threw out all his CDs. We just come and look at him."

The man smiled. The light was hitting his thick glasses in such a way that Lucy couldn't see his eyes. Dust motes sizzled in a beam of sunlight from the window. Some music was playing, loud and anxious-sounding. Lucy didn't recognize it.

"My uncle's a photographer. He has some photos he took of him a week before he killed himself."

Lucy felt her sinuses prickling with tears the way they did when she told Rosie scary stories. Her mouth felt dry.

"You can come see if you want," he said. He handed Lucy a card.

She put it in her pocket and crumpled it up there, so he couldn't see.

❧

One of Emerson Solo's CDs was called *Imago*. The title song was about a phantom limb.

She wondered if when you died it was like that. If you still believed your body was there and couldn't quite accept that it was gone. Or if someone you loved died, someone you were really close to, would they be like a phantom limb, still attached to you? Sometimes Rosie was like another of Lucy's limbs.

❧

Rosie was the one who went—not Lucy. Lucy was aware enough of her own desire to escape so she did not let herself succumb to it. But Rosie still believed she was just looking for ways to be happier.

❧

When Lucy got home from school and saw her sister's note she started to run. She ran out the door of thick, gray glass, down the cul-de-sac, across the big, busy street, against the light, dodging cars. She ran into the canyon. There was the place where the rattlesnake had blocked the girls' path, the turn in the road where they had seen the baby coyote, the grotto by the creek where the old tire swing used to be, where the high school kids went to smoke pot and drink beer. There was the rock garden that had been made by aliens from outer space and the big tree where Lucy had seen a man and a woman having sex in the branches early one Sunday morning. Lucy skidded down a slope causing an avalanche of pebbles. She took the fire road back down to the steep, quiet street. She got to the house just as Rosie knocked on the tall, narrow door.

Rosie was wearing a pink knit cap, a white frilly party dress that was too small, jeans, ruby slippers, purple ankle socks and a blue rhinestone pin in the shape of a large butterfly. No wonder people teased her at school, Lucy thought. She wanted to put her arms around Rosie, grab her hand and run but it was too late to leave because the man from the music store opened the door right away as if he had been waiting for them all that time.

He didn't ask them in but stood staring at them and twisting his mouth like he wanted to say something. But then another older man was standing at the top of the steep staircase. The girls couldn't see his face. He was whited-out with light.

Lucy knew two things. She knew that she and Rosie were going to go inside the house. She knew, too (when she saw it in a small alcove as she walked up the stairs), that she would take the screwdriver and put it in the pocket of her gray sweatshirt.

The walls were covered with plastic. So was all the furniture. Plastic was stretched taut across the floor. The walls were high, blond wood. There were skylights between the beams. Fuzzy afternoon sun shone down onto the plastic skins.

There was a long table. The older man stood at one end, watching. It was still hard to see what he looked like. The young man offered the girls pomegranate juice in small opalescent glasses. Lucy put her hand on Rosie's arm but her sister drank hers anyway.

Then Rosie walked out of the room.

"Rosie," Lucy whispered.

The young man said, "Do you know there's this dream that Jeffrey Dahmer had? He dreamed he was in this big, fancy hotel lobby with all these beautiful people wearing evening dresses and tuxedos. They were all pounding on the marble floor and screaming. But he was just standing there, not moving, not saying anything. He had on a leather jacket. He said it was like his skin."

Lucy felt for the screwdriver in her pocket. "I'm going to get my sister," she said.

But Rosie was back now. Her eyes looked brighter. She sat on a stool next to Lucy. She kept wetting her upper lip with her tongue.

The older man left the room.

"He's going to check on his photos," the

younger man said. "You didn't take anything, did you?"

Rosie shook her head, no.

"I have another story. It's about Richard Ramirez. When he went to this one lady's house, she kept him there like half an hour talking. Then he left. He didn't touch her. Do you know what she said to him? She said, 'My God, what happened to you?' And she listened. That was the main thing, she listened."

"What happened to you?" Lucy whispered.

The light in the room changed. It turned harsh. Emerson Solo was reclining on a chair. His skin was broken out, his hair was greasy, in his eyes, and he had a bottle in one hand. His long legs were stretched out in front of him. A blue butterfly was inside the bottle.

"Get the fuck out of here," the man from

the music store said, very softly. He was not looking at Lucy. The light was in his glasses. He was being swallowed up by the strange light.

Lucy felt the spell crack apart like an eggshell. She grabbed Rosie's hand. She pulled Rosie up from the stool. Rosie felt heavier, slower. Lucy dragged her sister out of the room. There was another staircase leading down to a back door.

Lucy flung herself down the staircase, pulling Rosie behind her.

"Lucy!" Rosie said.

A photograph had fallen out of Rosie's pocket. It was of Emerson Solo sitting on a chair with his legs stretched out in front of him.

Rosie tried to grab the photo but Lucy kept dragging her down the stairs. Their footsteps pounded, echoing through the house. Lucy fell against the door with her shoulder and jiggled the lock. The door opened.

They were in a strange, overgrown garden. Tearing through brambles. Lucy saw a crumbling stone staircase. She pulled Rosie down it, deeper into the bottom of the garden. A palm tree was wearing a dress of ivy. There was a broken swing moving back and forth. A white wrought iron bench looked as if it had been thrown against a barbed wire fence. The bougainvillea had grown over it, holding it suspended.

The barbed wire was very intricate, silvery. It was like metal thorns or jewelry. There was one small opening in the bottom. Lucy crawled through. Rosie followed her. But she stopped. Her ankle was wreathed in a circlet of silver spikes. Lucy dropped to the ground and carefully slipped the anklet off of her sister, not cutting her, not even catching her purple ankle socks.

She pulled Rosie to her feet. They were standing on the road, across from the wilds of the canyon. There were no cars. Not even the sound of cars. The sky was blue and cloudless. Lucy felt a buzzing sensation in her head like bees or neon.

She dragged Rosie across the road into the trees. The light kept buzzing around them.

Lucy reached into the pocket of her gray sweatshirt. It was empty. She reached into the other pocket and felt around. Nothing. The screwdriver was gone.

Gone, Lucy thought.

Rosie dropped to her knees on the soil.

"Lucy, look."

"What?" Lucy said. Her mouth felt numb, it was hard to talk.

"Blood roses."

"They don't grow here."

"I know that."

❧

The two sisters faced each other, waiting for the shivers to graze their arms, making the hairs stand up, but instead they felt only a strange, unnatural warmth as if spring had seeped into them and would stay there forever.

Giant

$\mathcal{S}$omething was wrong with Rachel Sorrow. Her limbs felt like sandbags, heavy enough to crush a small child. Her skin felt grainy. Her eyeballs strained with the intensity of a bulimic's and her mouth was dry. She lay with her head smashed against her bedroom door. Her feet against the opposite wall. Her neck ached, her fingers and toes tingled numbly. My, she had grown!

John Mandolin had chosen her to do his social studies project with him. It was about teenage suicide. They researched the topic together. She had gone over to his house after school. The magnolia trees were blooming big, waxy, white flowers. The eucalyptus trees were dripping their medicinal-smelling leaves onto the lawn. The light in his house was soft and melancholy. John Mandolin's parents weren't there, but his beautiful sister and her boyfriend were making out in her bedroom. Even the beauty of John Mandolin's sister intimidated Rachel Sorrow.

John Mandolin was sketching Rachel Sorrow as she sat on his bed under a David Bowie poster from the '70s. He was going to paint a portrait of her. She sat there wishing and wishing that she could be more beautiful.

Like her friend Berry Rodriguez. John Mandolin had a crush on Berry Rodriguez before he noticed Rachel Sorrow. Berry Rodriguez had a thick, long, brown ponytail and long brown legs. She almost never spoke. She scowled a lot. She was a brilliant ice-skater and rode horses on the weekends. Berry Rodriguez seemed more interested in horses than in boys, so John Mandolin had eventually given up on her. But Rachel Sorrow could not stop comparing herself to Berry Rodriguez whenever John Mandolin looked at her.

John Mandolin rode his bicycle everywhere. He had very developed leg muscles, not unlike Berry Rodriguez's. He had straight blond hair that fell into his eyes. Blue eyes. Like Rachel Sorrow, he never let them take his picture for the school yearbook but she was sure it was for a different reason. Some noble, anticonformist reason rather than because he thought he would look stupid.

John Mandolin was the most beautiful boy that Rachel Sorrow had ever seen, not to mention the most beautiful boy who had ever shown interest in her, let alone the most beautiful boy, by far (the only one, actually), who had ever kissed her.

But the kiss had made her feel so strange. As she drove home through the streets of the darkening valley she could barely see for the tears. They slid down the sides of her face, cold on her hot cheeks. They trickled into her mouth, tasting of salt. Maybe her own tears were the poison that made her grow.

The metallic Santa Anas were rustling the

palm fronds and eucalyptus. Maybe the electricity in the air had contributed to the spell.

Rachel Sorrow's friend Sasha Sorenson won biggest flirt in middle school. She had soft blond hair and pretty green eyes, little teeth that showed coyly when she smiled and big dimples. When they graduated from middle school, three boys pledged themselves to her in the class will and testament. She lived in a house with lots of glass walls and a pool. Her mother was a fashion designer and her stepfather was a photographer. She was always dressed in the cutest trendy clothes.

Rachel Sorrow's friend Elodie Sweet was tall and thin with dark skin and full lips and cascading gold-streaked brown curls. People said she could have been a model. She was a straight-A student and the best artist in her class. Like Sasha, she lived in a house with lots of glass walls and had a wardrobe so extensive that she and Sasha could wear matching styles every day of the week.

Sasha, Elodie and Berry went ice-skating at the mall after school. Then they sampled perfume at the department store counter and ate frozen yogurt at the ice cream place. On weekends they went horseback riding at the stables in the hills. Rachel Sorrow never joined them because she could not ice-skate or horseback ride.

Rachel Sorrow saw them at school and ate lunch with them in the quad. But it always felt as if they knew something she would never know, that they lived, somehow, in a private world of prismatic color, cherry lip gloss, shiny ice, frosty air and sleek-haunched creatures who knew more about sensuality than any boy. While Rachel Sorrow was turning into a giant.

Yes, that is what happened. After she returned home from John Mandolin's kiss she went into her bedroom, locked the door and began to grow.

The thickness of her limbs; oh, even her tongue felt thick! Her brain ached in her skull. Her heart had grown to be the size of a watermelon. It thudded heavily in her chest. (Unfortunately, the proportions of her body had not changed; she was still flat on top and a little pear-shaped through the hips.)

What are giantesses? Rachel Sorrow had once read a story about a race of magical beings, earth spirits, who were driven underground by mankind, where they festered and fell into corruption. Some shrank and shriveled almost to nothing and others grew grossly huge; unable to move freely they had to lie in the muck and mud, begging for someone to bring them roots and bones to gnaw on. Eventually they starved to death and the little people used their bones for shelter. Rachel Sorrow didn't know if she was one of these sorts of giantesses and what the deal was with John Mandolin. She wondered if he ever kissed her again, would that break the spell or make it worse? And, of course, he would never kiss her again, now. Even if Berry Rodriguez was not an obstacle (at least in Rachel Sorrow's mind). He would never paint her, he would never do a social studies project with her and he would never kiss her. She was revolting. She was much, much too much.

Giant

That was what her English teacher wrote on all her creative assignments, "Too much." Or at least, "A bit too much." Rachel Sorrow knew she was too much. She had way too many feelings. For instance, she was already in love with John Mandolin, just based on the fact that he had painterly talents, bicyclist's legs, the lips and heavy-lidded eyes of a Byzantine angel, and compassion for teenagers who contemplated suicide. If she and John Mandolin started dating, Rachel Sorrow would be compelled to write him love poetry every night. She would want to make out with him every night. She would climb in his window. She would weep into his shirt. He would say, "You are so intense. Like a storm. It's shocking how intense you are." She would get bigger and bigger every time they kissed until she crushed him with her lips and mashed him to bits with her teeth.

What, you may ask, became of this girl named Rachel Sorrow? Did she ever go back to her normal size? Did she shrink to the size of an elf and find a way to crawl into John Mandolin's pocket for the rest of her living days? Did she go storming through the halls of her high school, trampling the mean kids who called her names? Did John Mandolin graduate, go on a bicycle tour of the United States, settle down in Oregon and start a business hand painting racing bikes? Did he marry a giantess who lay with him in the countryside, her body his bed? Did he say, "You are too much, way, way, too much, go away, too intense, you feel more intensely about me than I will ever feel about you"? Or did he find a beautiful, sensitive woman his own size, someone who had learned to manage her emotions appropriately? What happened to Berry, Sasha and Elodie? Are they still friends? Were they one another's bridesmaids? In pastel dresses or black dresses? Did they go into medicine? Sports? The arts? Are they still married or divorced? How pretty are their daughters? How self-contained? When Rachel Sorrow grew huge, did her mother bring her supper on a tray like Max's mother in *Where the Wild Things Are*? Did Rachel Sorrow cry so many tears thinking of all these things, as well as of her great-grandmother's death in the Holocaust, that she drowned herself when she shrank to normal size, not unlike Alice in Wonderland? Did she shrink to normal size? Graduate? Fall in love? Get married? Have children? Divorce? Fall in love again?

What shall we do, all of us? All of us passionate girls who fear crushing the boys we love with our mouths like caverns of teeth, our mushrooming brains, our watermelon hearts?

My Haunted House

$\mathcal{F}$leurette believed that her doll-house was haunted. There had been a number of disturbing incidents. The tiny china plates from the glassed-in corner cabinet had all fallen on the floor and smashed. Which could have been attributed to an accident or a minor earthquake tremor but she was sure this was not the case.

The real electric lights would flicker on and

off at night. This could have been attributed to an electrical short but she was sure this was not the case.

When the dollhouse baby was found flung out on the floor, plastic limbs askew, Fleurette was sure that she was not mistaken.

Death lives in my dollhouse, thought Fleurette.

When she opened the front of the house, a cold draft blasted out at her. She ran to her mother, crying, but she could not articulate the problem. She was so sure her mother would not believe her. As a test, she told her mother stories all the time.

"There was a cow on the Petersons' lawn," she said.

"That's ridiculous," said her mother. "There are no cows in this neighborhood."

"I saw a blackbird with one blue eye."

"Fleurette, where did you get such an imagination?"

"My teacher eats chicken feet soup."

"Flurry, please stop telling tales," her mother said.

Can you imagine Mother's response to "My dollhouse is haunted; Death lives in my dollhouse"?

Fleurette knew it was useless to try.

Death could take many forms but in this case Death was a woman, very small, invisible, who lived in Fleurette's dollhouse. Death broke all the china plates because she did not need to eat and because it reminded her of earthquakes. She made the lights flicker because it reminded her of lightning. She considered lighting the birthday candles in the candelabra but if the house burned down she would have no place to live. Besides, she preferred cold temperatures. She did not believe in babies.

Fleurette had once loved that dollhouse. Her father had made it for her. He had even made most of the furniture. Fleurette and her mother had made the curtains and the pillows; they had wallpapered and carpeted. They had no idea that the tiny roses and fleur-de-lis and lace doilies and all the rest were decorations for Death.

Last Christmas the dollhouse family had a real Christmas tree and real birthday candles in the candelabra. Fleurette and her mother had wrapped tiny wooden blocks with shiny paper and thread to make presents. They made tiny stockings to hang on the mantelpiece and

tiny real dough cookies to put on a plate for
Santa Claus.

Fleurette's father was gone now. The dollhouse family still sat in the stasis of their
Christmas dinner. Except for the baby who had
been flung out of the house. Fleurette did not
have the heart to put him back. Instead, she
put him to sleep in a matchbox in her bedside
table drawer. He looked dead.

Fleurette's teacher had sent her to the
school nurse because she was bleeding. The
school nurse sent her to the school counselor
who called Fleurette's parents into her office.
Then Fleurette had to meet with another lady
who made her play with little dolls that
reminded her of her dollhouse family. There
was a mother, a father, a girl and a baby doll. A
little while after that, Fleurette's father went

away. Her mother said he was sick and he had to get better and then he would be back. Fleurette did not understand.

Fleurette went into the refrigerator and took out the pecan pie her mother had made. She scooped out the filling and ate it. It was creamy and tasted of burnt sugar. Then she ate a jar of pickles. Salty, crunchy. Then she ate some vanilla yogurt and a bag of rice cakes. Her tongue stung and her stomach felt full. But the food soothed her. It made her feel safe.

Meanwhile, Death was busy in the doll-house. Death had turned all the mirrors around on the walls. Death had torn all the pages out of the books. Death had ripped up the tiny reproductions of the Matisse and the Cézanne and the Monet. Death had let in some mice; they chewed on the furniture and pooped their little black mice turds on the carpets.

Fleurette begged her mother to throw the dollhouse away but her mother refused. So the dollhouse was moved to the garage where Death continued to live because Death must live somewhere, mustn't she?

*My Boyfriend
Is an Alien*

$\mathcal{M}$y boyfriend is an alien and this is a story about how I know.

I met my boyfriend while we were both photographing fires. The fires were sweeping the Santa Monica mountains and we had both parked on the Pacific Coast Highway at sunset to get some shots of the sky streaked with blood. My boyfriend was crouched in the brush with his camera. He had on a baseball cap over his shaved skull and little black-framed glasses. His shoulders were hunched protectively over the ribs that poked out under his T-shirt. Except for his eyes, he looked normal. But his eyes are much too big to be human. They are very long and wide. This is one way I know.

At the time my hair was pink and even though he pretended not to notice, it is my opinion that this attracted him to me, as aliens are interested in our colors, the way butterflies like certain flowers.

My boyfriend and I mumbled things about the fires but we didn't look directly at each other; we were looking at the sky. Then we skidded down the slope of rock and brush to get a different view. My photos looked like snapshots of a wildfire over a beach. His looked crazy beautiful, like the end of the world.

Afterward we went to eat burritos. My boyfriend had a carne asada burrito with extra hot sauce. I had a vegetarian bean and cheese with guacamole. My boyfriend is a carnivore. Aliens are not vegetarians. They like to eat cows cooked in various ways and other meats as well. He gnawed hungrily at his food and his big eyes flashed. I had mentioned that the fire photographs looked apocalyptic. He was telling me about the end of the world.

"The Mayan calendar ends on December 21, 2012," he said. "And it is so obvious that things are going in that direction. Look at your government! Look at the way they are treating nature and humanity! It is just so, so perverse."

I noticed that he didn't say our government. He had a slight accent but I couldn't figure out what it was. When I asked where he was from, he said, "All over. Far away." (!) His speech reminded me of poetry and sex.

"So what do you think will happen?" I asked, staring at his eyes. They were at least twice the size of mine.

"The world isn't necessarily going to explode. There will just be vast change. There is hope. It is in the rain forests, the healing plants from there, and in sex and the children who are being born. They have different strains of DNA. They aren't really human. So they will make the difference."

I didn't know what to say. Except I felt like fucking him when he said that. I took a bite of my burrito.

We went out other times. He always seemed to have cash. He took me to a little hole-in-the-wall Japanese place in West L.A. and ordered fried gizzard while I ate spinach with sesame seeds, a broiled rice ball, kabocha pumpkin, miso soup and lotus root.

"Do you know lotus root is supposed to be the food of the immortals?" I asked him. He tasted it respectfully but then went gleefully back to his gizzards.

This is one thing aliens like: animal flesh. They figure, why not? When in France . . . and all that. Besides, what is an organ that uses rocks to digest food when you are from outer space?

The first time we had sex was really something. My hair was bleached white. We were in the backseat of his 1965 VW bug at the beach. The stereo was playing Dead Can Dance. He likes that CD a lot. We were crunched into the backseat and he managed to get my clothes off without a struggle. I think he may have used his superpowers because one moment I was dressed and the next I wasn't. His own clothes came off the same way—baggy off-white cords and a black T-shirt that said "2012" on it, with an infinity symbol. He crushed into me with his body; it felt huge and heavy but also very light. I loved him so much at that moment. I wanted him to impregnate me with little alien babies but he was very conscientious with the condom. He put it on as gracefully and magically as the way he had undressed us. When he put himself inside me I started shaking and I couldn't stop. He was sweating all over me and he smelled like fire.

I didn't tell him that I had been hospitalized and that I had escaped. That I live with my crazy cousin and her boyfriend and a couple of

My Boyfriend Is an Alien

Hare Krishnas in a house in Venice. I didn't tell him that I've been diagnosed with schizophrenia or that I tried to kill myself with pills. That part of the reason I change my hair so often is so that I can forget who I really am. It didn't seem right to tell him these things. I didn't want to spoil the moment. We had such a good time when we were together.

Besides, when he touches me everything is okay. I don't want to hurt myself at all. I just want to kiss my alien boyfriend forever and ever. I need my body intact so I can do that.

I don't ask him about himself, either. He seems to prefer that. I don't know where he lives or where he gets his money. Once, when I hinted that I wanted to know more about his life, he said, "The only time is now. And now I'm here with you."

This time thing kind of drives me crazy. He never likes to make dates in advance. He says he doesn't understand our calendar; it doesn't make sense. He doesn't call me or email me but if I call him and ask him to come play with me, he always says yes.

Finally, one time, I said to him, "If there is a draft, will you take me to your planet?"

He said, "Sure, baby, whatever you want."

"Can I have your baby?" I asked him. "It would be so cute. It would have such big eyes!"

"We'll have to see about that," my boyfriend said.

"Maybe the condom will break," I said.

I've changed my hair again. It is black with bleached skunk stripes. Tomorrow we are leaving; I just know it. We are going to get away from this place before the whole experiment

explodes. We are going to get into his space-
ship and fly to his planet. He lives in the hol-
low core where no one can find us. Time is different there. The moment is so perfect in itself
that you don't need to think ahead or behind.
We will have little alien babies with big eyes,
big heads, big brains, big hearts that are filled
with compassion. On his planet there are no
words for schizophrenia, suicide or war.

That's where I'm going.

Horses Are a Girl's
Best Friend

$\mathscr{B}$erry liked animals more than humans. Who wouldn't? Animals don't see what you look like. They don't care. They respond to your essence. They value you for who, not what, you are. Berry was used to boys falling in love with her because of the shiny brown ponytail on the top of her head. Because of the sunny brown clear color of her skin. Because of the size of her breasts and the length of her legs. But none of the boys seemed to care about who she was inside. And even if they cared, they would have to go through so much to find out. They would have to ask her so many questions. Animals never ask questions; they just know.

Berry went horseback riding every week-end. She drove her VW bug on the freeway, into the hills of Hollywood. Into the trees. There were stables at Griffith Park and Berry rode her horse down the dusty trails. She wore Levi's and cowboy boots. She liked the feel of the animal, sleek and muscular between her thighs. She loved the warm-straw smell of the horse and the way he responded to her voice and her movements. Sometimes it really did seem as if they were one creature.

Her friends stopped coming with her. They were more interested in boys and shopping now. She liked to be away from their gossip and their chatter. And from her house, from her three brothers who were always taking the remote away and screaming at her to get out of the bathroom. They treated her like some kind of mutant who had invaded their world of baseball and automobiles with her distracting hair and torso. They put posters of skinny blondes in bikinis up on the doors of their rooms as one might put up crosses and bulbs of garlic to scare away vampires.

One day Berry was cantering along all alone. The sky was gray; the air smelled of smoke. Her ponytail bounced on her back. The city, with its people who saw you but didn't know you, who touched you but didn't feel you, who heard you but didn't understand you, was far away.

And then, there he was.

There he was and she would always remember him standing at the curve of the road with his black hair and his flared nostrils and his gap-toothed smile and his goatee and his sunglasses and his white undershirt. Just like any other boy. Except he wasn't.

Because he wasn't riding his horse.

They were silent for a while.

"You a Valley girl or what?"

"What?"

"You look a little like a Valley girl." He gestured to the top of her head where the ponytail was fastened with a scrunchy. "The . . . the thing."

"And who are you, homey?"

"East L.A., man."

"Uh-oh."

"What's that supposed to mean?"

"Big tough guy."

"Yeah, I'm tough. But I can be sweet. That's what the ladies tell me."

At this point he was not making a good impression. He was more man than animal and it didn't sit well.

It did cross her mind, though, if she were honest—it did cross her mind that it would be awkward but extremely interesting to have sex with him. She had not had sex with a boy before. Everyone thought she was a scared, uptight virgin but it really had to do with the issue that boys did not perceive essence and so, then, what was the point in making love, which was all about essence, or at least should be?

They rode for a while (rode, she thought, is that the right term?). He was whistling between his teeth—some song she had heard on KROQ or something. He even played a little air guitar without realizing he was doing it. She was jealous that he didn't need the use of his hands. His biceps were developed and the veins protruded a little along the ridge of muscle.

"So what do you do in the Valley, girl?"

"What do you do in the barrio, homes?"

"Hey!"

"Well!"

"Okay, what do you do?"

She shrugged, embarrassed all of a sudden. Like she should be embarrassed!

"Come on, tell me. I won't laugh at you."

"I ice-skate."

"Ooh, skater girl. You got the legs. What else? Do you go to the mall with your friends?"

"So?"

"I'm just asking. What do you want be when you grow up? An ice-skater? A cowgirl?"

"A vet," she said, not unaware of the way it might affect him.

"And I don't think you mean as in Vietnam. Desert Storm. Persian Gulf. Iraq."

"No, I mean like taking care of animals." She couldn't help emphasizing the last word. She thought he winced a little.

"Why that?" He was serious now and his voice was softer.

"I like them better than people. People don't shut up."

They rode silently for a while. He swatted a fly on his arm. His nostrils flared. His back haunches rippled.

"I have to go," she said.

"Okay, Doc. See you again sometime."

❧

They met every Saturday after that, in the same place on the trail. Miraculously, no one else was ever there. They rode in silence most times listening to their breath.

This was enough for her. In fact, this was better than anything. This was better than when he spoke and tried to be a man.

❧

He told her a few things, though. He told her that he had to stay in his mother's basement most of the time. That his family felt shame. But at the same time his hombres revered him in some way. They considered him their mascot, if a bit of a freak. They held their meetings in his red-lit basement. Drinking beer, playing cards, rapping and showing off tattoos. At one point they had all gotten matching tattoos of a man-horse somewhere on their backs.

One night she woke up and a man was standing in her room. Before she could scream out, someone had a hand over her mouth.

She thought, Not. Like. This.

The man said, "I won't hurt you. I'm with your friend. He got hurt real bad."

When she stopped struggling the man led her gently to the window. A truck was parked on the quiet street. The man shone a flashlight at the truck and someone inside put on another light for a second, long enough for Berry to see someone she recognized in the back of the truck.

He was bleeding from his flank. His eyes were glassy and his breathing shallow. She knelt beside him and ran her fingers across the bridge of his nose. It was broad with a little bump.

"No," she whispered.

"I'm going to be okay," he said. "You're going to fix me up and then we are going to be married and have all these little babies galloping around the house."

But he was weak by now. A pale sheen of sweat glazed his forehead. She said to his friends, "We have to call someone."

"No way. We can't call someone. Look at him. What are we supposed to say?"

She cleaned him up as best she could and they told her to sew up the wound but she was too scared. She'd never done anything like that. They said to use a needle and thread and they'd pour alcohol on it. He was delirious by this time. She was crying.

By morning he was gone. They drove away and she still had his blood on her hands. Later, she would tell herself it was a hallucination, all of it. How could it be real? There are no centaurs in Los Angeles. And gang members from the east side do not venture into the Valley to swear their love to even the loveliest of lonely girls.

Skin Art

*C*lodie Sweet did not think she would ever get a tattoo. Even when she fell in love with Darby who had a tattoo parlor on the east end of Melrose. She always imagined what people's tattoos would look like when they were seventy years old. The saggy inked flesh. It just didn't feel right to her.

Rachel said, "You might not even live that long."

Sasha said, "They have lasers that'll remove those things now. If you change your mind."

Elodie said, "The whole point is not to change your mind. It's supposed to be forever. That's the whole point."

Berry smirked primly; she would never get a tattoo!

Both Sasha and Elodie liked to wear startling clothes and they had even gotten their noses pierced. But tattoos were a different thing; you couldn't just let the skin grow back!

Darby had tattoos all over his arms and chest and back like a shirt. He had devils and angels and roses and lilies and serpents and tigers and dragons and scorpions and butterflies and bleeding hearts and skulls and mermaids.

Elodie had met Darby when she was shop-

ping on Melrose with Sasha. They were wearing their matching lace petticoats over black
tights and black combat boots. They saw Darby
at a magazine stand and were impressed by his
Mohawk. He asked to take their picture for his
MySpace page. Then he gave them his card and
showed them his tattoos. He and Elodie started
emailing each other after that. It turned out
they liked the same early punk bands, films
(*The Decline of Western Civilization* and *Blade
Runner*) and artists (she loved that he had Frida
Kahlo as one of his top MySpace friends).

Darby was from the Midwest but he'd gone
to art school in New York. Then he came to
L.A. and opened his tattoo parlor. Now he was
twenty-four. He told Elodie Sweet that she
was beautiful and had the perfect name but
was too young and that she should find a nice

underage guy to hang out with.

Elodie told Darby that age was only an abstraction, like time, and that what mattered was how two souls connected. Darby told Elodie that even having sex with her wasn't worth going to jail.

Elodie responded to this in a way that no one, not even her closest friends, ever would have expected. She stopped dressing up in outfits that matched Sasha's. She stopped listening to music and going shopping. She stopped ice-skating and horseback riding. She ate raw cookie dough and then went on long runs by herself in the hills to burn off the calories. She drew pictures of herself and Darby on adventures all over the city. It was an ongoing comic strip on its way to becoming a graphic novel. Except it had no plot. It was just Elodie and Darby being in love in different locations. On the carousel at the Santa Monica Pier. On the carousel in Griffith Park. In the fountain at the Hollywood Bowl. On the boardwalk at Venice Beach. At the Magic Castle and Yamashiro's restaurant in the low hills of Hollywood. At the Theatricum Botanicum in Topanga Canyon.

And then, a plot came to her.

Elodie woke up one morning with a tattoo. It was a tattoo of a red rose on her hipbone and on the densely clustering petals it said "Darby." Her first thought was that he had snuck in, in the middle of the night, drugged her and done it while she was sleeping. It looked just like his work. But how could she have slept through all that? And she didn't feel hung over or in pain. The tattoo had just materialized on her skin.

She showed it to Sasha who thought it was

cool and, because Sasha believed in those things due to her own rather improbable life, insisted that it was a manifestation.

"It happened by itself because you are so in love with him. Your body did it."

"I like the idea of him sneaking in my window and drugging me a lot better."

"Well, at least it's pretty and in a discreet place," Sasha said. "When you get a boyfriend you can cover up the name with another leaf."

I'm not going to get another boyfriend, Elodie thought, but she didn't say it. She believed tattoos were for keeps.

Days passed and she kept her rose hidden. It comforted her. At night she stood naked in front of the mirror looking at it. It emphasized her long torso and the slender curve of her hips. The privacy of her pelvis. It looked just like something Darby would have done. She wanted to email him and tell him but she knew it would sound too crazy.

Then one morning Elodie stepped out of the shower and caught a glimpse of color in the mirror.

It was a giant lotus blossom on her lower back.

She called Sasha. "This is getting creepy," Sasha said.

"Getting?"

"Yeah. This is really f-ing creepy."

"What am I supposed to do?"

"Is it pretty?" Sasha asked.

"It's gorgeous."

"I guess you don't do anything," Sasha said. "At least it's not a bong."

There was a D.A.R.E. urban legend that

was going around their school about a boy who got high and had his friend tattoo a picture of a bong on his chest. It was huge, lopsided, blurry and gruesomely ugly.

This did not make Elodie feel better.

She worked on her comic strip. In it, she started manifesting tattoos. At least it was a plot.

And in real life the tattoos kept coming. A Tibetan goddess was sitting cross-legged on the lotus flower. Butterflies swarmed around her. Stars hung over her head. Wild animals slept at her feet.

Elodie was not that big. The tattoos soon covered all of her slender back, shoulders and hips. One morning her arms wore lace sleeves. Morning glories and oleander blossoms were clambering over her shoulders toward her breasts. A pretty but lascivious-looking fairy with battish wings flew across her abdomen. Elodie put on a long-sleeved black turtleneck and drove out of the Valley, through Laurel Canyon, down Melrose to Darby's tattoo parlor.

He looked up at her when she walked through the door. He had bright blue eyes that felt invasive. The sides of his head were freshly shaved.

"Did you finally decide to let me do you?"

"Very funny," she said.

"Sorry. Tattoo you."

She stepped closer to him. The air conditioner in the store was broken and a little fan whirred. They were both sweating. Especially Elodie in the turtleneck. In the back room she could hear the buzz of someone's needle.

Elodie took off her shirt and flung her arms in the air. Her breasts were small and upturned, framed by flower tendrils. She pivoted around and then dropped her arms to her sides.

"Holy shit. Who did those?"

"I did."

"Put on your shirt," he said.

He took off his own and went to cover her with it. She pulled away from him.

"You could get me shut down," he said. He looked at his naked chest and put his shirt back on.

She put her hands over her face. Her back with its Tara, its garden, was shaking. He helped her put her shirt on again. He stood watching her, but not touching, like she was the goddess on her back come to life—beautiful but terrifying.

"Talk to me," he said.

(Every girl loves to hear those words from the right man. It is possible those words are the greatest seduction line ever. Especially if they are said without any ulterior motive, as Darby said them then.)

Elodie told him that the tattoos had appeared. "You better help me," she said. "At first I thought it was cool. Then I thought I was just going crazy. Now I'm scared they are going to grow onto my face. Onto my cheeks and lips! I'm not a freak!"

"Of course, you're not," he said gently.

"I can't help it if I want to be with you. It's not my fault."

"You are going to like a lot of guys, Elodie Sweet."

"Shut up! You're the freak. Shut up!"

"Come on," he said.

She followed him to his apartment in the hills of Silverlake. It was in a rickety little bungalow overlooking the water. A string of colored Christmas lights hung across the porch and there was an outdoor fireplace surrounded by bougainvillea. Inside, the walls were a collage of images torn from magazines. There were Balinese shadow puppets, conch shells, Buddha statues, Hindu goddesses, African carvings, candlesticks encrusted with wax drippings. His bed was in a corner, dimly lit, under a crowded bookshelf. She wondered if he ever worried about earthquakes.

It is amazing to think of how little it takes to make a girl, of a certain age and artistic temperament, believe she is in love.

"Come here," he said.

Skin Art

It was not exactly what she had hoped for or even expected. He was sweet but rough and he didn't look into her eyes. Afterward, he put on the TV. It was the Independent Film Channel, but still.

Elodie went home. The tattoos began vanishing, one by one, fading to stretch-mark-like shadows on her tawny skin and then nothing at all.

A year later, by the time she was away at college, even his name was gone.

My Mother the Vampire

At that time, Sasha did not know that she could sing. Sasha's house was like a Jetsons cartoon. The furniture was '60s space-age plastic. The lighting was low and frosty. Some of the light fixtures were shaped like stars and constellations. There were round chairs that spun in circles and big glass walls overlooking a kidney-shaped pool. Dreamy, lyricless music was always playing from speakers hidden in the walls. There was a fully stocked bar and a big screen TV. Everyone liked to hang out there. Elodie and Berry came over and the girls lay in the sun and painted their toenails. Sasha always used the most extreme shades of nail polish. She liked greenish black and neon orange. Elodie liked deep reds and Berry liked neutrals. They drank diet sodas and ate salads with iceberg lettuce, cherry tomatoes and Thousand Island dressing. Sometimes they invited boys over. The boys all had a crush on Sasha because Elodie and Berry were not interested in them but Sasha always gave them her biggest dimpled grin and lifted her breezy hair to let them put suntan lotion on her back. They did goofy dives off the diving board and threatened to pull the string of her bikini top. They raided her kitchen for chips, salsa and beer. Elodie and Berry rolled their eyes but Sasha just gave them her smile again, peeking out at them from under strands of blond hair as she painted her tiny toenails vile colors that managed, on Sasha, to appear coy and cute.

One of the boys was named Clyde Carrera. He had thin brown hair that was always falling into his olive green eyes, a long face and a dimple in his chin. He had a little crackly voice that sounded like it was changing from a boy's voice to a man's, but never quite did. Sasha sometimes let him paint her toenails or give her back rubs and sometimes she even kissed him but then she sent him away saying she just wasn't ready. Clyde Carrera liked Sasha so much that he did what she asked, went home, masturbated with a pair of underpants that he had stolen from her drawer, and then came back to put suntan lotion on her skin and let her put his hair in pigtails if she wanted.

Sasha's mom, Bets, was rarely around so the kids could go wild at Sasha's house. Bets was a former model. She was rather shockingly beautiful. Black hair flowed to her waist. Her eyes were a violent blue. Everyone assumed she did a lot of Botox and Restylane. She looked more like Sasha's sister, especially when she was dressed in her Juicy sweats or her baby doll tops with jeans and ballet flats, her hair in a ponytail. In fact, people would often say, "Is that your sister?" It made Sasha uncomfortable.

Sasha's mother said things like, "Sasha is so pretty. She's really got the looks. Luckily, because she struggles with other things. Like school. But looks will get you far in this world."

She said these things in front of Sasha, and sometimes to strangers.

Once she said them in front of Clyde Carrera who got drunk and told Sasha her mother was a bitch and he wanted to rescue Sasha from her and bring her home to live with him and sleep in his baby sister's room.

Sasha told Clyde never to call her mother names. She told him not to bother coming back to swim in her mother's kidney-shaped pool and drink her mother's beer ever again.

&

Sasha lost a lot of weight and her friends were worried that she might be bulimic because as far as they could see she was always eating. She ate pizza and steak and french fries and donut holes. She even switched from diet sodas to regular. But she was getting skinnier and skinnier and there were dark shadows under her eyes like eye shadow put on upside down. Sasha promised her friends that she wasn't vomiting behind closed doors in the mirror-paneled bathroom. She said she just had a high metabolism, like her mother, and told them not to worry.

Clyde Carrera came over late one summer night with flowers—daisies and orange lilies. The warm air made the scent of the flowers and the chlorine from the pool more intense. Through the glass walls the water glowed with its own blue haze. Bets was out as usual and Sasha was alone, wearing a boy's T-shirt and fuzzy slippers shaped like white cats and watching a Madonna concert.

Sasha wondered what it would be like to have Madonna as your mother. She loved

Madonna's wardrobe and how she trans-
formed herself all the time and how she
adopted a baby from Malawi. She knew that
Madonna had a special machine at home that
gave her oxygen facials so she would never
look old.

Sasha let Clyde in because the Madonna
concert was depressing her, because of the
flowers and because she missed putting his
hair in pigtails. She gave him a beer and he fed
her Cherry Garcia ice cream from her mother's
freezer, out of the carton with a turquoise plastic spoon. He said he thought she should stop
losing weight, that she was just perfect. Then
he gave her a foot massage that made her
squeal with pleasure and almost made him
come. Clyde kissed Sasha's feet, her ankles,
her slim calves and thighs. She whispered, "I

know you picked those flowers from my mother's garden," before she let him kiss her farther up.

It was like a transfusion.

❧

Every night after Sasha turned thirteen Bets came to her daughter's bedside. Bets hummed a little tune as she tied the tourniquet around Sasha's slender arm. Then Bets patted Sasha until a frail blue vein stood out and Bets stuck the needle in. It didn't hurt much. There was usually only a tiny speck of blood where the needle went in and rarely a bruise. Afterward, Bets gave Sasha a Hello Kitty, Barbie or Disney Princess Band-Aid and a lollipop. Sasha's tongue was orange or green or bright red and she had bright sugared bits stuck in her molars. The dentist began finding a lot of cavities so Sasha started getting up and brushing her teeth after the lollipop, although her mother never suggested this. By then, Bets was asleep, next to Sasha in Sasha's double bed.

She slept like a languid teenager, well-fed on her daughter's vivifying fluids.

Clyde wanted to take Sasha away with him when he graduated and moved to Seattle to go to art school. She said she couldn't leave her mother. Clyde emailed her for a while but when she stopped writing back he gave up and dated Marcy Parks who was physically Sasha's exact opposite and who he would later marry.

Sasha seemed like such a sweet girl with such a nice upbringing. Yes, her mother was a little narcissistic but so are other L.A. moms and not all their daughters start shooting heroin at nineteen. No one could understand either (though they were impressed) when, at twenty-seven, having cleaned up her act, Sasha became the head of the needle exchange program in downtown Los Angeles.

By then, Sasha had finally moved out of her mother's house. She got a cottage in Silverlake with roses in the courtyard and sunny windows. All of the furniture was from thrift stores and looked nothing like something out of a cartoon. Sasha spent a lot of time alone recording songs she had written and putting them up online. They were catchy tunes, reminiscent of the early eighties. People said Sasha's voice was a little like a happy Debbie Harry's. In spite of the upbeat sound the lyrics were frustratingly obscure and dark. But the more depressing the lyrics Sasha wrote, the happier she felt.

Sasha never really blamed Bets. She understood and, after all, someday she might be a mother, too. It is hard to be a pretty girl in this world. It is hard to be a woman growing old.

Wounds and Wings

*A*udrey found him by the side of the road after his girlfriend had left him. The wings were torn off at the shoulder but they were perfectly intact. There was blood only at the place they had been. She put him in her mother's SUV and took him home.

She cleaned and bandaged his wounds. She had never seen anyone's eyes look so sad. The sadness was not hidden by anger or pride or

Francesca Lia Block

fear; it was just raw sadness.

She gave him some chocolate chip cookies she had made but he only looked at them as if they were bad art. She washed his bloody clothes and let him sleep on her bed with the down quilt covered in pink roses while she slept on the futon. At night he growled in his sleep, gnashed his teeth and threw the rose-covered pillows off the bed.

She decided to call him Sad Lincoln because of his long, sad face and his long, thin body. She went to a thrift store and bought him some thermal long-sleeved shirts and flannel shirts and baggy corduroy pants with the pile only slightly worn down at the knees. The black lace-up boots he had been wearing when she found him on the side of the road were still good but the T-shirt was bloodied and besides he no longer needed the holes ripped out on either shoulder for the wings.

He went for days without eating and then wolfed down waffles and scrambled eggs, potato salad and cheese sandwiches, grilled chicken, steamed broccoli and pie. He surfed the internet and downloaded music that he played for Audrey when she got home from school. It was usually apocalypse rock, grim and sexy. He also liked to design logos with her graphics program and look up websites that dealt with supernatural phenomena. He kept her room clean, fixed her computer and did her chores for her in secret while her parents were at work. Sometimes when she found him at the computer, he was wearing her clothes— her beads and scarves and sweatshirts. Once she woke up in the middle of the night and saw him sitting at her bedside watching her face.

The wounds on his shoulders healed without stitches, leaving scars she longed, but didn't dare, to touch. Except for the time she had tended his wounds she never touched him. Once he brushed against her and she started crying uncontrollably and for no apparent reason. After that he was extra careful and she had no words to explain why she wanted to cry like that again.

She kept him hidden in her room all day, and at night, when her parents were asleep, she took him outside. He told her stories about himself. He told her about the lands where he and his brother ate fruit off the trees and slid naked down waterfalls. He told about his mother who looked like "that actress. Who is that actress?" when he saw *Breakfast at*

Tiffany's with her and she said, "Audrey Hepburn?" and he said, "She has your name? Cool! Yes, her. She looked like that!" and about his stern father with the single eyebrow like his own who ate the marrow from the ox bones and soup made of chicken feet and didn't understand how doing art could be anyone's actual paid work.

Lincoln didn't say much about the girl-friend ("her," "she," as if it were unbearable to say her name), the one who had torn off his wings with her bare hands. Audrey wanted to know her name and see a picture of her but then she didn't. She imagined that the girlfriend looked like the model in the catalogue that she found him gazing at one day, the woman with the cropped platinum hair, the round, dimple-smile face, bronzed, glimmering skin and supernaturally green eyes. He quickly made a comment about how Audrey would look cute in those platforms ("big shoes" he called them), as if he didn't want to hurt her feelings by staring at models. It was scary to realize that he might care that much about her feelings. Who was he anyway? It could never work out. She had found him at the side of the road! He never left her house! He had wings! Well, once he had wings.

She didn't ask him about the wings, because she sensed he was self-conscious about them. It would have been like asking someone about their pimples, even though she thought the wings, and the scars from where the wings were, were beautiful. She did wonder about them, though. She wondered how they got there. She wondered if his mother had them, if "she" had them. One night when they were sitting in the garden listening to the summer crickets and the sprinklers tossing wet glitter in the moonlight, he told her that he was embarrassed when he was in high school. She asked why and he said, "Well, you know, how teenagers are always embarrassed. You've got zits, greasy hair, too much hair, whatever." (Now he had dreadlocks as if in defiance.) That was all he said but somehow she understood that he was referring to the wings and that they had not been something that anyone else had in the place he came from, wherever that was.

Audrey had painful, ugly cystic acne when she was fourteen but her mom took her to a good dermatologist who gave her a really strong medication with pictures of deformed babies on the seal of each pill. Now her skin was clear, so it was worth it. She only had a couple of scars. One was by her mouth and she wondered if it would bother the first boy she kissed. She planned on getting a laser peel when she was older. There were also some studies linking the drug to depression but Audrey wondered how you could tell, when people with acne tended to be depressed anyway.

When she was thirteen, Audrey's mother came into the bathroom while she was in the tub and said, "Oh, your little mound of Venus is sprouting," and it made Audrey so sick that she wanted to throw up all over her mother. She wondered if he had been born with the wings or if they had sprouted during his adolescence, if it had hurt as well as frightened him and if he was grateful to the girlfriend on some level for ripping them off. It was one thing to have hair and pimples but they were normal, they were what everyone had and so it was much less disturbing than growing something completely foreign.

Audrey's period did not delight her either. She found it shocking and, frankly, humiliating to have blood coming out of her vagina. What if she bled through her clothes in public? She'd seen a girl once with a red stain on her white lace skirt and everyone laughed. She imagined that Lincoln would understand this sense of shame, about something taboo but secretly beautiful and empowering, better than most boys because of the wings.

Audrey had a relatively sane mother and father who loved her. She had a nice house to live in and food to eat and cute clothes to wear. She was not exceptional looking but she was pretty enough now that her skin had cleared up and she had what people might call a pleasant if slightly gummy smile, a chic, short, layered hairstyle and a slim body that she liked to dress up in vintage dresses and cowboy boots. She didn't have too many friends, but that was okay; she had books and DVDs and she did well in school and now she had Lincoln. It didn't make that much sense that she felt as wounded as she did.

But she realized that even wounds were okay because maybe the wounds were why she and Lincoln had found each other.

Lincoln eventually got a job designing and managing websites and doing some graphic art gigs on the side, all from Audrey's bedroom. He gave Audrey money for groceries and flowers and marijuana and big shoes. He still never left the house but she had to go to school every day. She applied to a local junior college, in spite of the fact that her parents wanted her to go to an Ivy League school, so she could live at home and be with him.

She missed Lincoln so much during the times she was away that her saliva dried up and her stomach clenched emptily. It was always a relief when she came home to him. Like water or food. Like music or that moment when you cut yourself with a knife and squeeze the skin and no blood oozes out.

Changelings

$\mathcal{H}$e didn't see Daisy at first. Not until his dad died of a brain tumor and his girlfriend, Natasha, was killed in a car accident six months after that.

Daisy told him later, "Your brain can only see what it believes is real, Kissy Face. I was here all along."

She had long, wild hair that always seemed to be tangled up with leaves and sticky buds and she rode around on a skateboard as if it were the marker on the Ouija board she kept in her enormous backpack. She wore little kids' faded T-shirts from the thrift shop. One was a green Hulk shirt; one pale pink one with two people silhouetted on a beach said "Rio de Janeiro, Brazil: Land of Lovers." She had a *Wizard of Oz* T-shirt and a hot pink one that said "The Ramones" with all of their names in a circle. "Johnny Joey Dee Dee Tommy." With the T-shirts she wore black miniskirts and black boots and black tights cut off at the feet so they were always running up her leg in revealing, shredded strips like ladders. Her eyes changed color every day.

His dad had the headaches and then they were all sitting in the living room and his mom was crying and his dad was saying words but the boy didn't really hear him. Except he got that his dad had a mass in his brain and would die within the year. Cancer was something all of their brains understood. It was part of their history and you heard about it all the time on TV.

His mom and dad were best friends. They almost never saw anyone else. He couldn't imagine his mom without his dad. They were like one entity. Their idea of a big night was cooking a gourmet meal together (something with figs, something with polenta, pomegranate seeds, salmon), drinking a glass of wine and getting in bed by nine. They had not slept apart one night since they got married twenty-two years ago.

The tumor was inoperable and his dad died faster than even the doctors predicted. His mom became a zombie after that. (His brain knew and recognized zombies from watching old horror movies.)

Natasha had straight, long, brown hair and wide-apart green eyes that were just flooded with light. She always wore moss green Puma sneakers and baggy clothes as if she were trying to hide her beauty, which of course made her seem even more beautiful. She might not have even noticed him if his dad hadn't died, so it was his loss that woke her up just as the loss of Natasha woke him up to see Daisy.

Natasha started emailing him and then they went to the mall and saw *Pan's Labyrinth* and ate a burrito at the Mexican place and avocado roll sushi at the Japanese place and soft-serve ice cream. Natasha reminded him of a cat with her eyes, shiny hair and graceful body.

She had freckles and a merry, slightly manic giggle. She was a ballerina and always walked with her toes out. These are the things he learned on their mall date: Her favorite food was waffles with whipped cream and strawberries. Her favorite book was called *The Fairies* and had girls dressed up in wings photographed as if they were the real thing. Natasha believed in fairies with a conviction that did not match her usual laid-back manner. Her eyes would light up even more than usual and she would talk about them breathlessly and with longing, though she had a superstition about not calling them by name.

Once she grabbed his arm so hard it hurt.

"She's one!" Natasha whispered.

"Ouch! What?"

"One of *them*!"

"What? Who? Ouch, Tash." He didn't see who she was pointing at.

"You only see them if your brain believes they are there," she said, a bit impatiently. "But I never thought they rode skateboards!"

Later, he thought she must have been talking about Daisy, of course.

He believed in death because he had grown up watching it on TV and then his dad had died and that made it really real. He believed in Natasha's death in a car accident with a drunk driver at the ski resort she was visiting with her family because he had never fully believed that she was his girlfriend to begin with. He knew that Natasha's death was real, but he could not accept it. He thought about her all the time. He listened to the Tori Amos CD she had burned for him. He read her books and her journal. Her mother had given him the journal. Natasha mentioned him casually, describing where they went and what they saw. She called him cute once. She said she felt sorry for him. He imagined that her mother had not read that part carefully, or she would probably not have given him the journal, would she? In Natasha's journal, also, was an elaborate description of what "they" were.

"They were earth spirits, part of nature. Elementals. So beautiful! But they were attacked by evil forces and retreated underground. They got sick and skinny. Some people say reptilian. A few of them tried to rescue their children from their own fate. They bravely ventured up above ground and left their babies in baskets on strangers' doorsteps, hoping for the best."

This is what he learned from Natasha and it is what Daisy explained to him as well. In fact, she had been one of those babies. Her parents had discovered her in a basket and called the authorities. Eventually they had chosen to adopt her. But they had no clue as to who she was. Daisy had a plan. She wanted to go find her true parents in their underground lair.

He said he would go with her. He would have done anything she asked him, of course. By then, he was in love with her. She had come to him in his greatest pain and loneliness; in fact, without his pain and loneliness, he knew she would never have come.

"I'm so fucked up," he had told her. "I'm depressed. I don't care about anything. I have ADD. I get bad grades. Even before my dad got sick I was fucked up."

He had never said these things to Natasha. He had not believed she would understand. He had believed she was going to leave him some-how, although he hadn't imagined it in the way it had happened.

Daisy said, "You are not fucked up, Yummy. Your world is fucked up. It is very fucked up. It is a very, very fuckity uppity world and you are just responding normally to its psychotic vibe. Do you hear me? Because this is very impor-tant. This is something you need to know in order to change."

"Where do you come from?" he asked in amazement, touching the twigs in her hair.

"From underground, Panda Bear," she said.

❧

The catacombs twisted beneath the canyon. Old stone rooms and tunnels. It smelled of mold and damp earth and worms. He followed her, the circle of her flashlight illuminating the turns in the passage.

They could hear music coming from up ahead, drums and flutes.

The passage opened out into a larger room. The people were gathered around in a circle of candlelight. One woman sat on a large chair made of stones and tree branches. She had branches in her hair like antlers and a dress of torn lace.

"That's the queen," Daisy said.

The queen grinned, baring her missing front teeth. She was a very thin creature with a long, bony face and glittery candle eyes. Next to her was, he supposed, the king. The king looked like a junkie rock star, sinewy with thin, straight pale hair and deep lines in his face. He had pockmarked cheeks with high bones, round, sensitive-looking nostrils and exaggerated lips. He wore an overcoat and large black boots without any laces. The king grinned, too.

The people gathered around. They put their frail, cold hands on the boy and on Daisy. Their skin reminded him of a snake he had once touched.

"Stay with us," they said.

"I have to go ask my mom," he said.

"She can come, too. Stay with us. We are prepared. There will be a revolution. Things are changing. You just must believe it, yes? You just must believe."

❧

The boy went back to talk to his mother. She was sitting in front of the television eating microwaved frozen pot stickers and a carton of Ben and Jerry's. He turned off the TV.

"Are you okay?"

She blinked at him, blotting the grease on her lips with a napkin. "Yes. Fine. And you? Did you eat? There's frozen mac and cheese. I was watching *Project Runway*."

"I know, Mom. It's important. I have things I wanted to tell you.

"I want to take you someplace. Underground. There's a girl I met. She's not from here. Her real family lives underground, under Laurel Canyon. They are like this different race. But they are cool. They want me to stay with them. I thought you might want to come. It doesn't seem good for you here anymore, without Dad?"

She blinked at him. Her eyes were red.

"Heidi Klum is so pretty, don't you think?" she said. "I wonder if that scar her husband has bothers her?"

He went outside. The night air felt damp on his skin. He could smell the tinge of meaty dinners and fireplaces. Some people already had put a ring of ghosts made from sheets and broomsticks around their tree and there were uncarved pumpkins on porches. Daisy had said they could be goblins on Halloween.

"What does a goblin look like, exactly?" he asked.

"A fairy who has lived underground too long. A corrupt-looking fairy."

"I can't dress up like a fairy," he said. "I mean, that word, you know?"

"I know. That's messed up. That we can't use that word. How is eldritch? Is that better?

More manly? Anyway, Toughy, you get to change out of that same flannel shirt and those cords and be a goblin. Goblins are cool."

He wondered if they had Hershey bars underground. If they carved out pumpkins, scooping out gobs of stringy insides and seeds with their bare hands before putting the candles in. Could he listen to his iPod? He wondered if he could stay with Daisy, sleep in the same bed with her. Were there rules about things like that? He had not been inside of her yet but she had gone down on him and swallowed his come in her mouth. When he had reached inside her black stockings she was wet and slippery and she smelled like the flowers at Natasha's funeral.

She called him different names in between kisses. "Cosmonaut. Smooshy. Mister. Mister

Slick. Creamsicle."

He did not think that there was anything wrong with him. That he was delusional or psychotic or even depressed. The world is fucked up, he thought to himself. He cried a lot now. Daisy told him it was a good thing.

"Let the pain wash over you," she said. "Let the pain teach you. If you can feel it then you can feel joy again, Candy Bar. I mean, Manly Candy Bar. You are a very manly candy bar. Real men cry, you know."

He realized how much he had changed.